No More Yawning!

For my sister Coral - Paeony Lewis

Welcome to the world, Charlie! - Brita Granström

First published in the United Kingdom in 2008 by Chicken House,
2 Palmer Street, Frome, Somerset BA11 1DS.
www.doublecluck.com

Library of Congress Cataloging-in-Publication Data
Lewis, Paeony.
No more yawning / Paeony Lewis ; [illustrated by] Brita Granström.—1st American ed.
p. cm.
Summary: Florence and her toy monkey Arnold try to fall asleep but Florence's big yawns keep
them awake. Includes tips for falling asleep.

ISBN-13: 978-0-545-02957-5
ISBN-10: 0-545-02957-0

[1. Bedtime—Fiction. 2. Sleep—Fiction. 3. Toys—Fiction.] I. Granström, Brita, ill. II. Title.

PZ7.L58763Ns 2008
[E]—dc22
2007015257

10 9 8 7 6 5 4 3 2 1   08 09 10 11 12

Printed in Singapore
First American edition, March 2008

Body text was set in Coop Forged.
Display text was set in Block Berthold.

Book design by Ian Butterworth and Leyah Jensen

No More Yawning!

By **PAEONY LEWIS**

Illustrated by **BRITA GRANSTRÖM**

Chicken House

SCHOLASTIC INC./New York

I'm Florence.
This is my drawing of Arnold in a banana bed.
I'm getting him into a sleepy mood because
it's seven o'clock and time for bed.

Mom kisses me good night and
dims my light. I yawn
a **big, BIG** yawn and
shut my eyes.

I yawn again. This time my yawn's
so **BIG**, it's bigger than a banana.

We're *trying* to
sleep, we *really* are,
but we can't. The trouble is, Mom
forgot to give Arnold a good-night kiss.

We find Mom. Mom kisses Arnold. I kiss Mom.

Arnold wants another kiss.

"No more kissing. No more yawning,"

Mom says. "It's time for sleep."

We're *trying* to **sleep**, we *really* are.
But Arnold's feeling lonely so I sing him a lullaby
about a twinkling star. Arnold
likes it so much, I have to
sing it five times.

Then I have to draw him a picture of a

shiny
bright
star.

All the singing makes me thirsty. So I go to find Mom.

Mom gives me a cup of water and I only spill a bit when I yawn a yawn BIGGER than Arnold's smile.

Mom says, "No more singing.

No more yawning.

It's time for sleep."

smile

yawn

We're *trying* to **sleep**, we *really* are. But Arnold wants a story. He says it *has* to be about a monkey and a giant banana tree.

I hunt through all my books, but I can't find that story. So I make it up. Though telling a story isn't easy when you can't stop **yawning**.

giant **BIG** tree ↑

happy monkey

Arnold wants pictures, too.
So I start drawing.

Oops, Mom's seen my bedroom light. I jump into bed and yawn a yawn BIGGER than Arnold's tummy.

Mom frowns at all the books and says,
"No more stories. No more yawning. It's time for sleep."
But we're *trying* to sleep, we *really* are.
Mom tells me I'll get sleepy if I count imaginary sheep jumping over a gate.

yawn

Arnold

tummy

sheep

So I try counting sheep.

One, two, three, four. Six? Five? I've got it wrong.

Sometimes I play with cutout numbers, so tonight I make cutout sheep. I number them. One, two, three, four, five, six, seven . . .

What's after seven? Arnold thinks it's nine. It's hard to count sheep when you can't stop **yawning**.
Nine, ten, eleven, twelve . . .

What's after twelve? I don't know. Arnold doesn't know. We have to ask Mom.

I **yawn** a **yawn** BIGGER than Arnold's tail to show Mom that we're *trying* to **sleep**, we *really* are. It's not our fault numbers are so hard.

MY BIG YawN

Mom groans and says, "No more counting, no more drawing, no more cutting, no more yawning. It's time for sleep."

She tells me I'll get sleepy if I shut my eyes and think of everything that's yellow. And if I'm still not asleep I can choose another color. Then another.

I shut my eyes tight.

Sun. Butter. My yellow chair.

Grandpa's hat. Sunflowers. Buttercups. Cheese. Our car.

What else is yellow?

Bananas!

We're *trying* to **sleep**, we *really* are. But I can't think of anything else that's yellow. Arnold can't, either. So we think about pink.

My curtains are very pink. And cotton candy. Raspberry milkshakes. Pink socks. What else? Are my big yawns pink? We're not sure. I call out to ask Mom.

Mom is mad. She says:
"No more kissing.
No more singing.
No more stories.
No more counting.
No more drawing.
No more cutting.
No more colors.

We're *trying* to **sleep**, we *really* are.
But it's hard to sleep when you're sad.

Mom says sorry for shouting and
gives me a hug. And Arnold, too.

I ask Mom how she got to
sleep when she was little.

Mom thinks hard. Then she
remembers. She'd shut her
eyes and make up a
story in her head.
Soon she'd be
dreaming about
fairies or digging
up treasure.

I tell Mom my dream story will be
about exploring a jungle full of monkeys,
bananas, wild animals . . .
I yawn a yawn BIGGER than
Arnold and shut my eyes. . . .

monkeys

bananas

wild animals

We *were* asleep, we *really* were. Totally, completely asleep. Then Mom woke *us* up with a noisy yawn as **big** as an **elephant!** Naughty Mommy!

elephant

noisy yawn↑

I tell Mom, "No more yawning. It's time you went to sleep!"

And I give her a kiss. "Good night!"

Tips on Falling to Sleep

Mom thinks I'm a NUISANCE at bedtime. I think that having to sleep for twelve hours is the NUISANCE. Unfortunately, I'm told I HAVE to sleep because that's when my body grows and my brain takes a break and my mom rests, too. So here are some more tips from me and Mom on getting to sleep.

NO NAPS

When I was very little, I needed a nap in the afternoon. Now it stops me from sleeping at night if I fall asleep during the day. Though it's hard to keep my eyes from closing when Mom starts chatting to a friend when we're out shopping.

LOTS OF EXERCISE

It's really hard to sleep when my body feels all fidgety and isn't tired. Mom says that happens when I haven't done much exercise, like swimming, biking, or tossing Arnold into trees in the park. Monkeys like swinging in trees, though sometimes Arnold leaps too high and once he stayed out all night until the wind blew him down. So I couldn't sleep then because I was so worried.

SOFT MUSIC

Sometimes it's noisy at night where I live. So I listen to a CD of soft music to help drown out voices and stuff. Arnold likes a CD that sounds like a storm in a banana rain forest.

REGULAR BEDTIME

Mom gets mad at Dad when he lets me stay up really late. She says I must always go to bed and wake up at the same time so that my body learns when it's time to sleep. I tell Mom that my body doesn't have a good memory.

RELAXING ROUTINE

Mom insists on a relaxing bedtime routine. That means no showers (they wake me up) or too much splashing in the bath. But sitting quietly in a warm bath with lavender bubbles is boring! After my bath, it's storytime. I like lots of stories, but Mom yawns after about six. Then it's bed and a kiss good night for Arnold and me.

NO SODA

Mom says most sodas contain caffeine, which will keep me awake and bouncy. So I drink warm milk and eat a plain cookie to relax me—*yawn!*

DARKNESS

I have thick curtains to keep out the light in summer. Though if it's too dark, then Arnold worries there's a gorilla hiding in the closet. So we have a dim night-light in case he wakes up at night. Arnold says it's like the moon shining in the jungle.

Grrrr...

Sweeeet Dreams!

Do you remember your dreams? As soon as I wake up, I think about my dreams. Then I grab paper and crayons and draw what I can remember (sometimes it's hard to remember). Here are some pictures I've stuck in my Dream Scrapbook. You could try it, too.

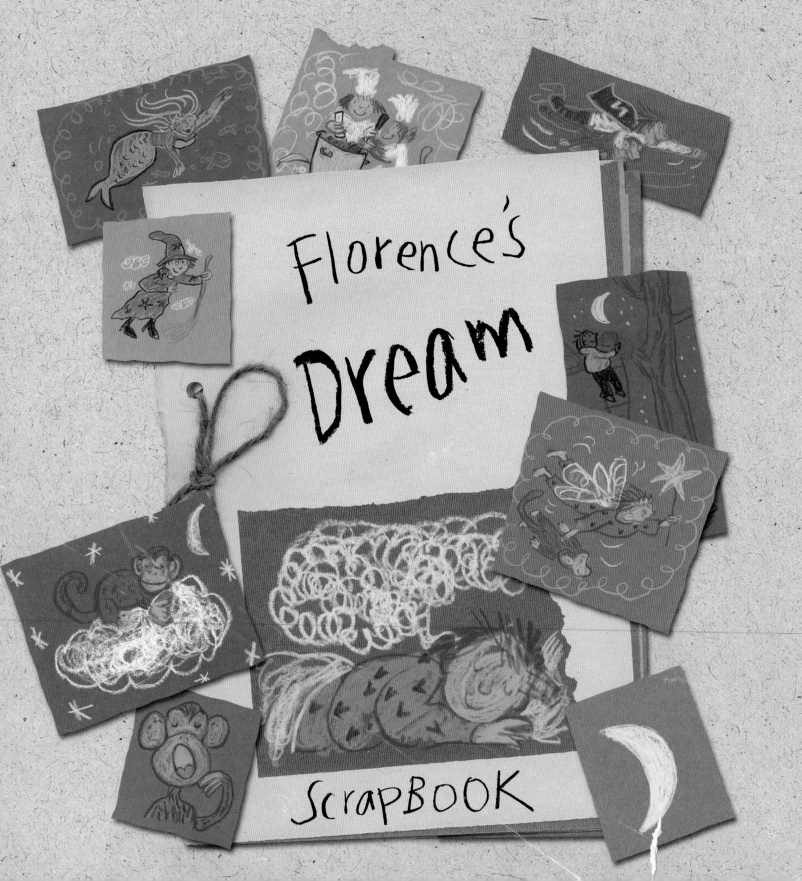

Florence's
Dream

ScrapBOOK